D1538421

MY 1ST GRAPHIC NOVEL®

The Forest Surprise

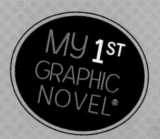

MY FIRST GRAPHIC NOVELS ARE PUBLISHED BY STONE ARCH BOOKS
A CAPSTONE IMPRINT
151 GOOD COUNSEL DRIVE, P.O. BOX 669
MANKATO, MINNESOTA 56002
WWW.CAPSTONEPUB.COM

Library of Congress Cataloging-in-Publication data is available on the
Library of Congress website.

ISBN: 978-1-4342-2520-7 (library binding)
ISBN: 978-1-4342-3064-5 (paperback)

Summary: Jake's forest hike is full of adventures and misadventures.

Art Director: **KAY FRASER**
Graphic Designer: **HILARY WACHOLZ**
Production Specialist: **MICHELLE BIEDSCHEID**

Photo Credits: Shutterstock: aleks.k, 25 (top); Brian Rome, 10; Cynthia Farmer, 25 (bottom);
fotomak, 6 (top); Hintau Aliaksei, 6 (bottom); irin-k, 16; Joshua Haviv, 21; Mark Winfrey, 7;
Martin Fischer, 20; Pakhnyushcha, 12, 14 (top); Paula Cobleigh, cover, 9, 23, 24, 29; skaljac, back
cover, 18, 22; Stanislav Bokach, 8; Svetlana Tikhonova, 13; Tereza Dvorak, 14 (bottom), 15, 16, 17;
Paul Clarke, 4, 5, 12

Printed in the United States of America in Stevens Point, Wisconsin.
042014
008172R

The Forest Surprise

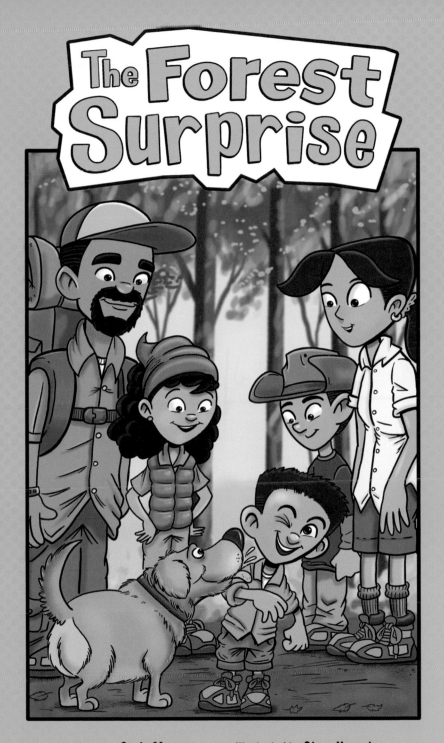

written by **Carla Mooney**   illustrated by **Steve Harpster**

STONE ARCH BOOKS
a capstone imprint

HOW TO READ A GRAPHIC NOVEL

Graphic novels are easy to read. Boxes called panels show you how to follow the story. Look at the panels from left to right and top to bottom.

Read the word boxes and word balloons from left to right as well. Don't forget the sound and action words in the pictures.

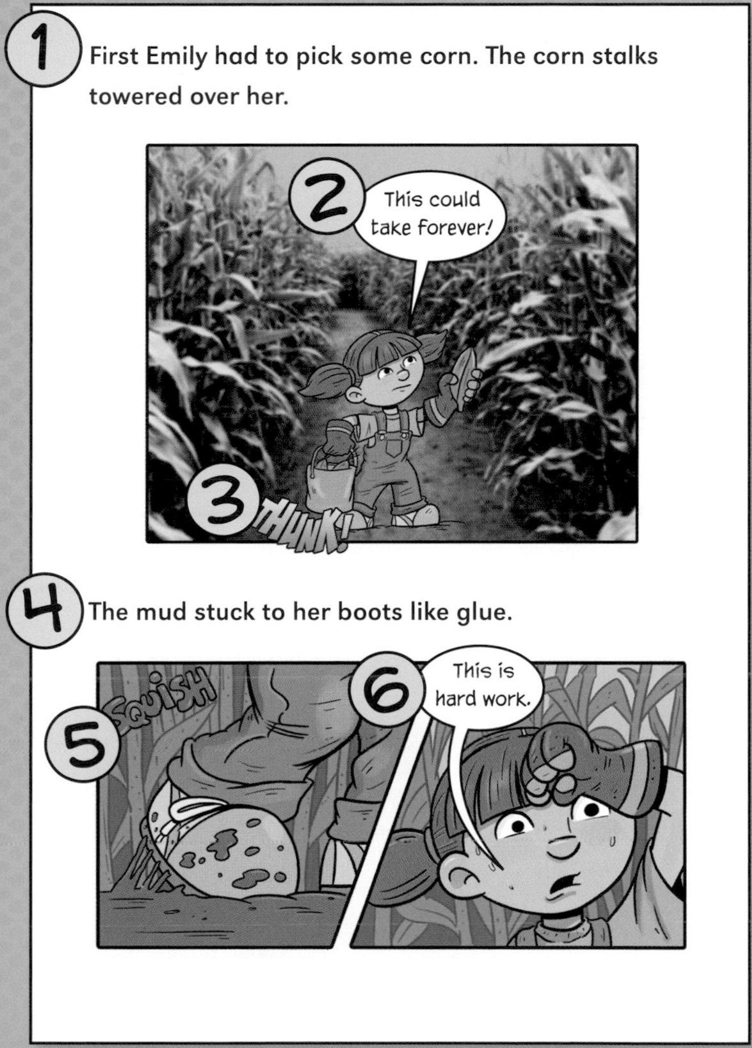
1
First Emily had to pick some corn. The corn stalks towered over her.
2
This could take forever!
3
THUNK!
4
The mud stuck to her boots like glue.
5
SQUISH
6
This is hard work.

The pictures and the words work together to tell the whole story.

Jake looked out the window. It was a perfect summer day.

He put on his hiking boots and grabbed his backpack.

Jake was ready for an exciting forest adventure!

At the forest, Jake found a hiking trail. Everyone followed Jake because he had a compass.

They hiked through trees and bushes. The path was covered in leaves, sticks, and rocks.

The trail was steep. Jake huffed and puffed. His legs were tired.

Jake sat on a rock to rest. He heard a loud cracking sound. He pulled out his compass.

Jake grabbed his water and kept going. He was not going to let one small problem ruin his day.

On the trail, Jake saw a fallen log.

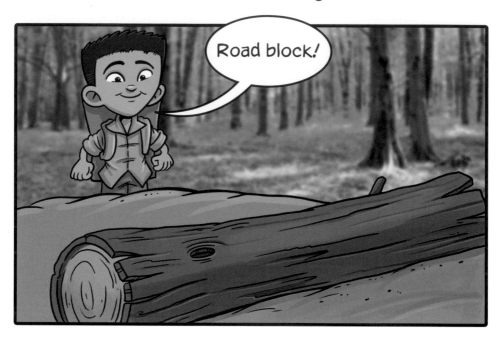

Jake climbed on top of it while everyone else walked around.

The log wiggled. Jake wobbled.

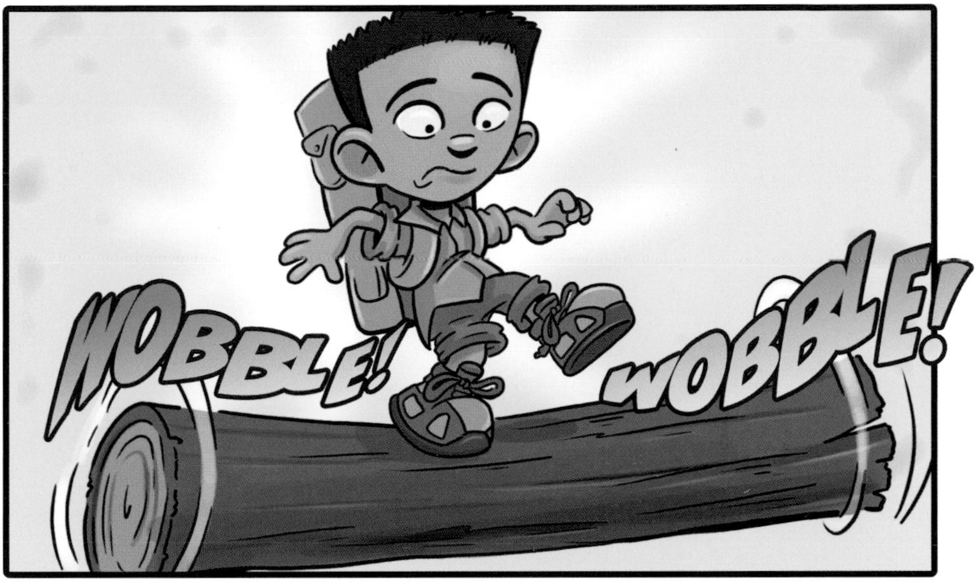
WOBBLE!
WOBBLE!

His feet slipped, and he landed in a mud puddle.

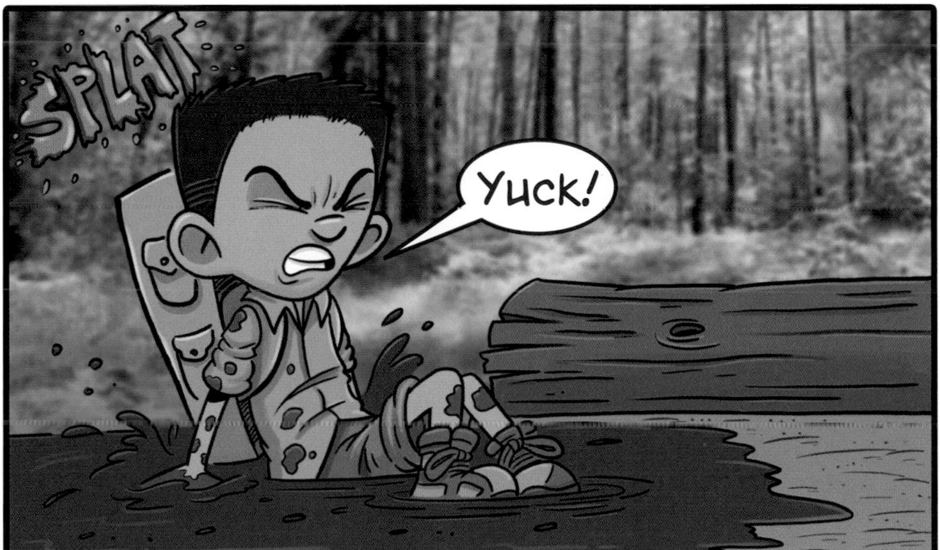
SPLAT
YUCK!

After drying off, Jake was hungry.

Mom spread a picnic blanket on the ground.
She unpacked sandwiches and lemonade.

Lunchtime!

Everyone else was ready to eat, but Jake still had to clean up his mess. He put his sandwich on the blanket.

While Jake cleaned up, a chipmunk tiptoed across the blanket. Jake did not see him.

The chipmunk liked peanut butter and jelly sandwiches, too!

After lunch, the family had a scavenger hunt. Jake was not happy about it.

Jake's sister spotted a squirrel racing up a tree.

His brother saw a snake sliding by a bush.

Jake saw a lot of deer.

He found a lizard. Neither animal started with the letter "S."

Suddenly Jake's dog, Max, stopped on the trail and barked. Then Max dashed into the bushes.

Max had found an animal, too.

When Max raced back to the trail, Jake knew what animal Max had found.

He could not see it, but he could smell it!

Max had found a skunk!

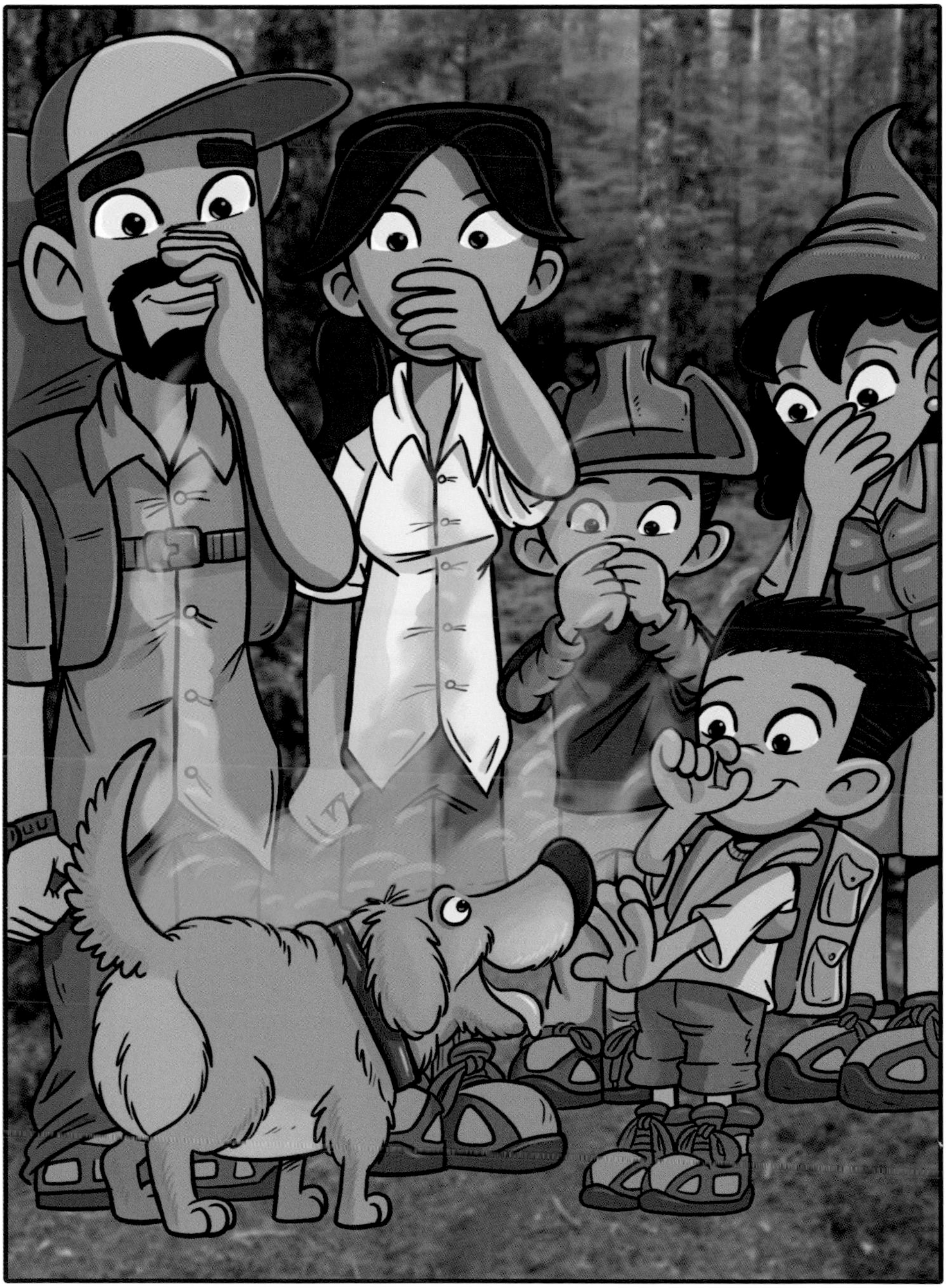

Soon it was time to go home. Jake's forest adventure was full of surprises.

Jake would always remember the sights and smells of his forest trip!

BIOGRAPHIES

CARLA MOONEY writes fiction and nonfiction on all sorts of subjects. She lives in Pennsylvania with her husband and three children. When she's not writing, Carla loves reading a new book and hanging out with her family.

STEVE HARPSTER loved drawing funny cartoons, mean monsters, and goofy gadgets since he was able to pick up a pencil. Now he does it for a living. Steve lives in Columbus, Ohio, with his wonderful wife, Karen, and their sheepdog, Doodle.

GLOSSARY

COMPASS (KUHM-puhss) — a tool that helps you find which way to go

HIKE (HIKE) — a long walk in the woods

RUIN (ROO-in) — to spoil or wreck something

SCAVENGER HUNT (SKAV-uhnj-er HUHNT) — a game where you search for a certain object

STEEP (STEEP) — sharply sloping up or down

TIPTOED (TIP-tohd) — walked very quietly on the tips of the toes

Jake's Guide to a Happy Hike

1. Wear proper hiking gear. (Be sure to pack a few extra clothing items in case you fall in the mud.)

2. Bring a compass and wear it around your neck. (This way you won't sit on it and break it.)

3. Watch your step, and do not climb on logs or loose rocks. (Or you may end up in the mud.)

4. Keep your food next to you at all times. (Or you may lose it to a chipmunk.)

5. Most importantly, stay away from skunks!

I ♥ HIKING!

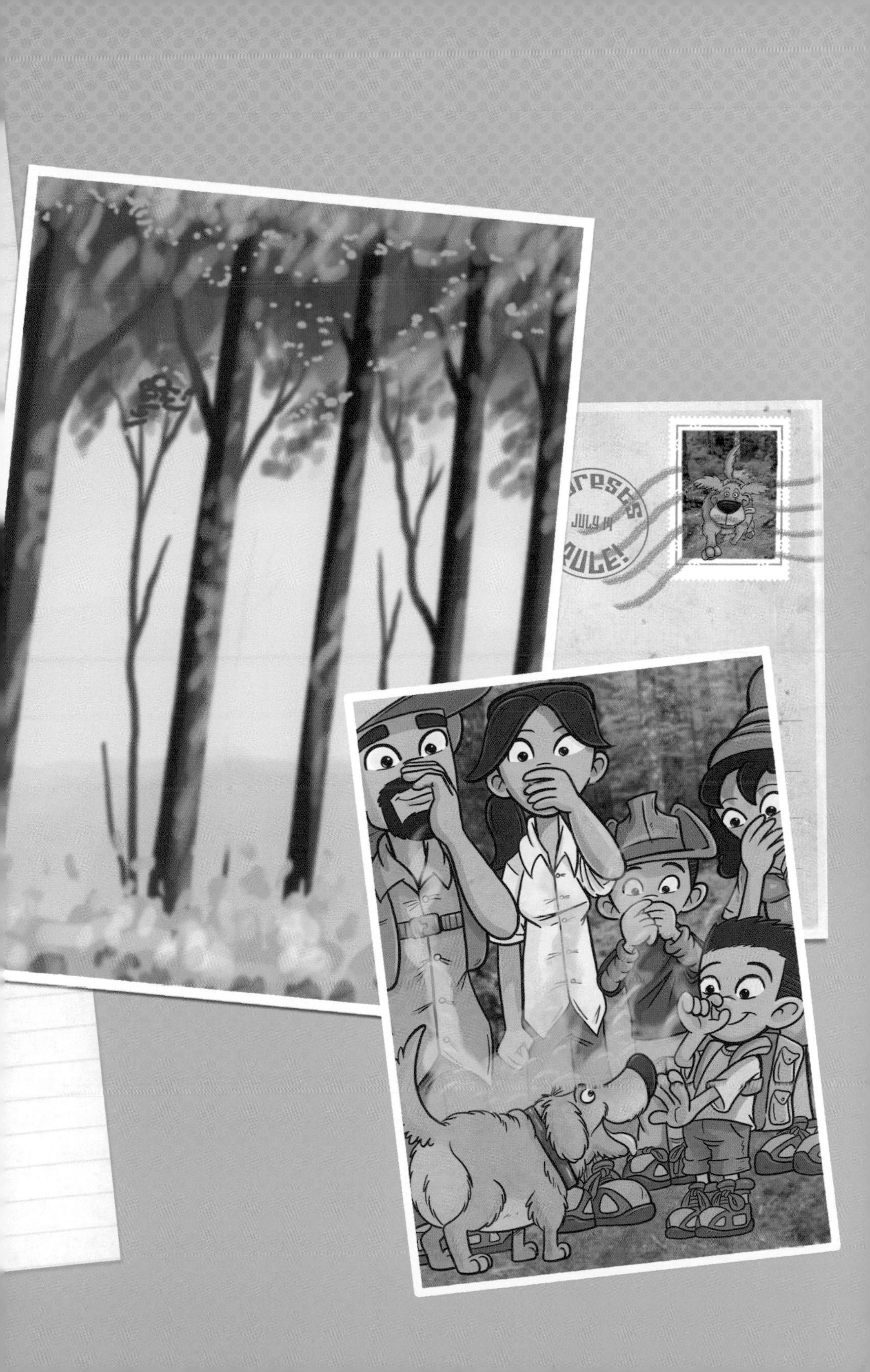

JULY 14
RULE!

DISCUSSION QUESTIONS

1. Jake is excited to visit the forest. What would you like to do on a forest trip?

2. What would you do if you got sprayed by a skunk?

3. Jake's day does not turn out the way he thought it would. Did you ever have a day that was different than you had hoped? Did you still have fun?

WRITING PROMPTS

1. Jake saw many animals in the forest. Draw a picture of an animal you would like to see in the forest.

2. Jake took his compass and backpack to the forest. Make a list of other items that might be good for a trip to the forest.

3. Jake's hike is harder than he thought it would be. Write a short paragraph about something you have done that was hard for you.